Accessing Kingdom Mysteries

Osita Eze

Ukiyoto Publishing

All global publishing rights are held by

Ukiyoto Publishing

Published in 2023

Content Copyright © Osita Eze

ISBN 9789357872706

All rights reserved.
No part of this publication may be reproduced, transmitted, or stored in a retrieval system, in any form by any means, electronic, mechanical, photocopying, recording or otherwise, without the prior permission of the publisher.

The moral rights of the author have been asserted.

This book is sold subject to the condition that it shall not by way of trade or otherwise, be lent, resold, hired out or otherwise circulated, without the publisher's prior consent, in any form of binding or cover other than that in which it is published.

www.ukiyoto.com

Preface

Sometimes in February 2006, the Lord led me to begin an intensive study on the mysteries of His kingdom. This was after I had stumbled on His words in Luke 8:10. It says: *"And he said, Unto you, it is given to know the mysteries of the kingdom of God: but to others in parables; that seeing they might not see, and hearing they might not understand"*. These words made a very profound impression on my spirit. As I continued to meditate on them, I concluded that God's kingdom is full of mysteries and that He wants believers to know these mysteries. Hallelujah! Since then, I have continued to search the scriptures to ascertain God's motive for revealing His kingdom mysteries to Christians. God has been so faithful in teaching me these mysteries. The truths revealed in this book are products of those studies.

This book is written to teach believers how to have access to God's kingdom mysteries. I believe that you will also receive all that the Lord has freely given to you as you receive the words revealed in this book.

Contents

Kingdom Mysteries	1
Custodians Of Revealed Kingdom Mysteries	3
How God Reveals His Mysteries	5
Why God Reveals His Mysteries	8
About the Author	*13*

Kingdom Mysteries

Kingdom mysteries are truths and deep secrets about the operations of the kingdom of God. They are teachings and instructions on the nature and growth of God's kingdom. They are infallible spiritual realities that God has ordained to be revealed to the saints for the fulfilment of His eternal purposes on earth.

Types of Kingdom Mysteries

There are two types of kingdom mysteries in the scriptures. They are:

(1). The Unrevealed Mysteries

(2). The Revealed Mysteries

1. **The Unrevealed Mysteries**: Unrevealed mysteries are truths or secrets that God has never made known to any man and might never reveal to any person no matter how minute they are. They are 'secret things' and they belong absolutely to Him (Deuteronomy 29:29a).

The closest example of this type of secret in the Bible is found in Genesis 25: 20-23 and Romans 9:9-13. These scriptures recorded that Rebecca had difficulty in conceiving children. Her husband, Isaac prayed to God on her behalf. God heard his prayer and she conceived twins in her womb. The children in her womb struggled together within her. This made her enquire from the Lord about them. The Lord told her that there are two nations in her womb and that the elder shall serve the younger brother. The scriptures reveal clearly that it was God's eternal counsel that Esau would serve Jacob, his younger brother-He took this decision before they were conceived in their mother's womb. The reason for God's choice of Jacob over Esau is unknown and unrevealed.

Another example of unrevealed secrets is found in 2 Kings 4:8-37. Prophet Elisha and Gehazi, his servant were regular visitors to the house of a certain notable Shunemite couple. On a particular day when Elisha visited the couple, he prophesied that the Shunemite woman will conceive and give birth to a son. This prophecy came to pass. Unfortunately, the child born to this family died after some years. Prophet Elisha knew nothing about the child's impending death until his mother came to announce it to him. To show his ignorance, Elisha made this statement: *The LORD has hidden it from me, and has not told me"*. God kept him in the dark about the child's death.

Please note that God does not always reveal all He knows about a situation to His children. He reveals only what is necessary for your survival and perfection. He keeps other details about a matter to Himself. When this happens, all you can do is to accept and obey all that He has revealed to you and forget about all other issues that He has decided to keep away from you.

2. **The Revealed Mysteries**: Revealed mysteries are secrets or truths that are divinely revealed. They are God's clear principles for living and conquest on earth. They address issues that concern all areas of life.

God will not always keep you in the dark about 'top' kingdom secrets that you need to know on issues that concern you and your generation. He reveals them to you in His time and season-He has carefully planned your life and has programmed it into His calendar. He reveals His will to you when the time is right.

What He has revealed and will reveal in the days to come are not only for you. They are for your children also (be it spiritual or biological). They are treasures that must be guarded jealously and with a high sense of commitment to God. Any person who carries these secrets in his or her heart and does them occupies a special place in God's heart. He or she will be the apple of His eyes and his or her security is guaranteed by Him.

These secrets are often generational and must be shared with all that you have begotten in the Christian faith (Deuteronomy 29:29b). They must be passed on to the next generation of Christians (Deuteronomy 6:6-9, 2 Timothy 2:2).

Custodians Of Revealed Kingdom Mysteries

God is a mysterious God. He is full of secrets and His ways are unsearchable (Isaiah 40:28). No one can have a full understanding of His secrets except they are revealed to him or her by God. Only the righteous and God-fearing persons have access to these secrets.

The secret of the Lord is with those who fear Him, and He will show them his covenant (Psalm 25:14)

...but his secret is with the righteous (Proverbs 3:32b, KJV)

Who Is A Righteous Man?

A righteous man is a person who does not walk in the counsel of the ungodly, nor stands in the path of sinners, nor sits in the seat of the scornful. He is a man who delights in doing the law of the Lord and in meditating in it always. He speaks the truth in his heart, does not backbite with his tongue against his neighbour, does no evil to a neighbour, does not receive or take up a reproach against his neighbour, honours them that fears the Lord, does not lend out money to people with interest, has clean hands and a pure heart. He shows kindness to all without fanfare.

Examples Of Righteous Persons In The Scriptures

There are several examples of righteous men and women in the Bible whom God revealed His secrets to. One of such persons is the prophets.

Prophets were in the Old Testament the only ministers who preached or taught the people of God by inspired utterance and revelation. They were the only preachers or ministers the people had. They were the only persons who could speak for God as they were inspired by Him. They were also called *seers* because they could *see* into the realm of the spirit and *know* things supernaturally through the gift of discernment of spirits, words of knowledge and wisdom. They were God's eyes and mouth-piece on earth.

Surely the Lord GOD does nothing, without revealing his secret to his servants the prophets (Amos 3:7, RSV).

God was 'almost' helpless when there was no prophet to hear Him out. He loved to fellowship with them because they occupied a special position in His heart. They were His spokesmen. They were the custodians of His secrets, covenants and plans. They were carriers of heavenly news. This was the reason their safety and security was guaranteed. They shook their world because of whom and what they knew-They knew God and had a personal relationship with Him.

Another example of righteous persons in the Bible is the New Testament Church. Every true follower of Jesus Christ is a member of the New Testament Church. He or she is entitled to knowing and understanding the mysteries of God's kingdom (Luke 8:10).

The New Testament Church is the body of believers who have been called out from the world by God to live as His people on earth under the authority of Jesus Christ. It is also the total of all the saints in the world whose sins have been washed away by the blood of Jesus Christ through faith and repentance from sins.

In this dispensation of grace, God has made the Church, which is you and I, the *"stewards of the mysteries of God" (1 Corinthians 4:1).* He has chosen to reveal His manifold wisdom which has been hidden from the world from the beginning of creation to you and through you. It is a royal privilege to be called a custodian of His mysteries.

Understanding and knowing His mysteries is yours by kingdom right. They are yours to possess. Go to God in repentance and possess what truly belongs to you. They are freely given to you by God through the Holy Spirit. Every Spirit and Word-filled believer has access to them. It is reserved for God-fearing men and women like you. Go for yours now.

How God Reveals His Mysteries

The knowledge of God's kingdom mysteries comes to you mainly by revelation. God reveals truths that are unknown to you by showing and by speaking to you about them through different mediums. Three main mediums shall be discussed in this chapter. They are through:

(1). Daily Divine Visitations

(2). Daily Personal Pursuit of God

(3). External Influence

(1). **Daily Divine Visitations**: To teach His ways to a believer, the Lord makes personal efforts to visit him daily especially in the early hours of the morning when there are no distractions to awaken his ears to receive clear instructions and revelations for that day. He wakes him up to give him his daily spiritual meal. This spiritual meal fortifies him against the darts of sin and builds in him spiritual stamina. He teaches him how to speak and what to say to the weary, ignorant and simple-minded people. Each daily divine visit presents the believer an opportunity to grow in character and spirituality.

Several persons mightily used of God in the scriptures were men and women who hosted God daily in their private closet for fellowships. They were persons who obeyed God and carried out His commands faithfully. God revealed Himself to them through the authoritative voice of His Spirit, visions and dreams of events yet to come. Examples of persons who had a daily thriving relationship with God were Moses, Samuel and Jesus Christ (See Numbers 12: 6-8, 1 Samuel 3: 21, John 5:19-20).

(2). **Daily Personal Pursuit of God**: God wants you to seek Him daily. He has assured you that if you seek Him with the whole of your heart daily, He will show you excellent things that you do not know. In this case, you have the primary responsibility of initiating a strong commitment to doing God's will and fellowshipping with Him daily. You must appear before Him each day with hunger and thirst for Him. Our fathers of faith sought God whole-heartedly and He revealed His will to them. Our generation will also obtain access to God's kingdom mysteries if we seek Him with all our hearts.

Call to Me, and I will answer you, and show you great and mighty things, which you do not know (Jeremiah 33:3)

Draw near to God and He will draw near to you (James 4:8a)

In the place of daily fellowship, you have an opportunity to ask God questions on life issues that you do not understand or even scriptures that you find difficult to comprehend. The twelve apostles out of curiosity and desire to know more about God's kingdom went to Jesus for the explanations to the parable of the sower which He had narrated to the multitude. They knew that there was more to be known from that parable and they wanted to know its interpretation. The Lord Jesus saw their readiness to know more about God's kingdom and He explained to them all that they needed to know about God's kingdom principles in that parable (Luke 8:4-15). You must note that our Lord Jesus did not make the attempt to show them God's kingdom mysteries *first*. The disciples sought for these mysteries *first* before Jesus revealed them to His disciples.

Another example of this is found in Daniel 2:14-23. King Nebuchadnezzar had a dream in the night which he had long forgotten. In the morning, he summoned all his advisers and wise men and commanded them to tell him his dream and its interpretation. Failure to do so would attract death for each of them. Daniel, a friend of the all-knowing God and one of the king's wise men requested the king to give them more time to find out his dream and its interpretation. He went up to God in prayers to seek His mercies concerning this matter. God had mercy on him and revealed the secret to Daniel that night. God alone can reveal hidden secrets.

He reveals deep and secret things; He knows what is in the darkness, and light dwells with Him (Daniel 2:22)

To receive anything (including divine secrets on any matter) from God, you must draw near to Him with faith in our hearts and He will give you the desires of your heart (Matthew 7:7-8).

(3). **Through External Influence**: Sometimes, God sends His ministers to you to explain things that you do not fully understand or have prior knowledge of. These ministers provide the missing link between what God had said about you or His kingdom and what He is saying about you now.

Sometimes, the Lord sends a believer to another believer to help him confirm His promises for his life and to reassure him of certain truths that He had earlier explained to him. He does not want us to be a people without clarity of mind and focus. That is why He sends people to us to teach us His secrets. Apostle Paul during his conversion was informed about God's call upon his life in Acts 9. He went about his daily itinerary with that consciousness. In Acts 13, God used the prophets and teachers in Paul's local church to confirm His call on his life and send him forth into the mission field. God spoke to our fathers through prophets and He still speaks to us through ordinary men and women who make themselves available to Him (2 Chronicles 20:20b).

Why God Reveals His Mysteries

There are four main reasons why God reveal His mysteries to you. They are:

(1). He is relational

(2). He wants you to know them

(3). He wants you to do them

(4). He wants you to preach and teach them to people

(1). **He is relational**: God is a relational being-He created you for fellowship. He wants a growing relationship and fellowship with you.

God began to fellowship with a human being from the beginning of creation. He visited the first man, Adam at the cool of the evening regularly. It was at the place of fellowship that God revealed to Adam his responsibilities on earth and showed him His daily provisions for him. Each of the spectacular experiences Adam had in the Garden of Eden was obtained through the fellowship he had with God. Unfortunately, Adam later lost all his God-given privileges because he lost his relationship with God. There were no more secrets to be shared with him by God because of the presence of sin in his life.

From the time of Noah and till now, God has always been searching for men and women, boys and girls with the right heart to fellowship with. He found Noah, Enoch, Abraham, Isaac, Jacob, Joseph, Moses, Joshua, David and many other persons through whom He revealed His intentions and secrets for their generation. He still wants many friends on earth. Dare to be one of them. He is looking for those who would be loyal to Him. Loyalty to Him sustains His relationship with you.

(2). **He wants you to know them**: God had hidden His mysteries from the princes and rulers of this world for your glorification even before the foundation of the earth was laid (Luke 8:10, 1 Corinthians

2:6-7). No eye has seen, no ear has heard and no human mind has conceived what God has prepared for you. He has prepared great revelations for you and is revealing them to you for your knowledge by His Spirit for one reason: *that you might know the things that have been freely given to you by God* (1 Corinthians 2:12).

The knowledge of the mysteries of God's kingdom is God's gift to you. It bequeaths to you the privileged position of being God's friend and confidant.

3. **He wants you to do them**: The most important reason why God reveals His mysteries and gives clear instructions to you is that He wants you to do them. Let us look at Deuteronomy 29:29b again. It says: "*...but those things which are revealed belong to us and our children forever, that we MAY DO ALL the words of this law*". God will only show His secrets to you and your children if He is sure that you will do them (Genesis 18:17-19). He will not hide them from responsible parents in the Lord.

God also reveals His mysteries to you because He wants you to take precautions or to inform other people about an impending danger. An example of this is found in 2 Kings 6:8-10. The king of Syria planned to fight a war against Israel. God revealed his strategies to Elisha, the prophet. Elisha warned the king of Israel of the impending danger and instructed him on what to do to remain in safety. Israel was thus saved from sudden warfare and loss of lives through the revelation given to Elisha.

Every word received from God must be received with meekness. You must be a doer of the word and not a hearer only. It is only those who continue to obey God's word that will receive His blessings and become a blessing to others (James 1:22-25).

4. **He wants you to preach and teach them to people**: God reveals His mysteries to you through the Holy Spirit so that you can preach and teach them to the unbelievers. The reason is this: He wants the unbelievers to become fellow heirs of His kingdom. He wants them to be members of the Body of Christ and partakers of His promise in Christ Jesus through the gospel (See Ephesians 3:4-13).

The preached gospel of Christ is the power of God (1 Corinthians 1:18). It liberates every person that believes it from the shackles of sin. Through it, God reveals His righteousness to the just (Romans 1:16-17). However, it is important to state that as simple as the gospel of Christ might seem, it is not believed by all when preached because it seems foolish to the perishing souls. It does not sound logical to the mind. It is not to be analyzed. It is to be received into the heart by faith and preached from house to house and in public places.

God reveals His mysteries to you because He wants you to know, do and preach them to the unbelievers. Learn all you can about His mysteries and pass on to the next generation all that He has revealed to you. He wants other persons to hear about them too.

Last Words

The journey to accessing God's kingdom mysteries begins with the act of submitting one's heart and will to the Lordship of Jesus. In case you have not surrendered to the Lordship of Jesus, this is an opportunity you must not miss. Say this prayer with me: Father, I recognize that I am a sinner. I repent of all my sins. I ask you to forgive and cleanse me with the blood of Jesus. I commit my whole life and heart to Jesus Christ. From this day forward, I belong to Jesus. Thank you because I know I am saved and my name is written in the Book of life.

If you have prayed this prayer sincerely, I say 'Congratulation' to you. You are now a part of the most loving family on the earth-the family of God. I would love to hear from you, pray with you, or give you further clarification. You can contact me through the following:

E-mail: eze_osita@yahoo.com, ezeosita1017@gmail.com

Call/ Whatsapp: +2347033341017

God's Revealed Mysteries Belongs To You

'*Accessing Kingdom Mysteries*' is written out of a great passion to help you discover how you can access everything that God has freely given to you.

In this book, you will discover:
- The meaning of kingdom mysteries.
- The foundation for obtaining kingdom mysteries.
- Reasons for the revelation of kingdom mysteries.
- How God reveals kingdom mysteries to Christians

It is a treasure for anyone who wants to enjoy the depth of God's riches.

About the Author

Osita Eze

Osita Eze is the Youth Pastor of The Redeemed Christian Church of God, Faith Sanctuary, Ondo, Ondo State, Nigeria. He is passionate about raising godly labourers especially among youths and young adults.

He is also a tutor at Hallmark Secondary School, Ondo. He is happily married to Sister Faith and they are blessed with a daughter.

www.ingramcontent.com/pod-product-compliance
Lightning Source LLC
LaVergne TN
LVHW041604070526
838199LV00047B/2129